AARON
A. LEHMAN

MYSTERY ON
DOG ISLAND

2005

Mystery On Dog Island

To Winnie

Acknowledgements:

Pauline Auger- Aboriginal Education teacher

Keith Denoncourt- "Essential Guide To Wilderness Survival", Outdoor Education teacher.

Helen Gall- Sketches

Kelly Harlton- Wildside Wilderness Connection.

Cathie and Robert Jensen- Proof reading

Trudie Moon- Computer

Terry Mosher - Editing

CHAPTER 1

Grease! Raymond had grease everywhere. He had smears of the slippery, gooey stuff on his hands and face and stuck in his long, black hair. Grease decorated the walls, dripped from the ceiling and a black slime oozed from cracks in the floor of the old, two car garage, revealing a history of wrecked cars waiting for repairs. Even the cracked windows on the big overhead door, that drooped on one side, had grease spots. The smell of exhaust filled the air.

Mom's not going to be happy about the grease on my pants, Raymond thought. *Why should I care? Good mechanics just get greasy and I love it.*

Raymond knew he could get this relic of a snowmobile running and that meant everything to him. The ripped, two man seat and the broken windshield didn't really matter. He had used all of his summer wages to buy this old, pull start model from a trapper friend. Happy to have an engine of his own to work on, Raymond met the challenge head on.

"Raymond!" Emily called as she burst into the garage. "Supper!" She came running toward Raymond and grabbed him around the legs as she often did. Too late.

Raymond reached down to pull her off and then he saw the big, black finger marks he left on her white tights.

"Emily! Get out of here! Leave me alone!"

Emily, with big tears and greasy tights, went crying to her mother.

Rats. Now I've hurt her feelings.

He didn't really want to hurt her, but this gem of a six year old just always seemed to get him into trouble. Emily, Raymond's little half sister, belonged to Rose and Allen. Raymond's mother, Rose, and his real father, Johnny, who lived north of Slave Lake in the northern lakes district, were treaty Cree Indians.

"Raymond! You get in here right now!" Rose called.

Raymond tried to clean up some of the greasy mess before he went for supper, but he knew he wouldn't make it in time. He put the carburetor and fuel filter back into the box of spare parts and threw his wrenches into the cluttered tool box. He grabbed an old rag to wipe his hands as he walked from the garage to the kitchen.

"Picking on little girls again?" Larry sneered. Larry was Raymond's step brother, who was always looking for a fight. This mouthy, blond, twelve year old son of Allen made Raymond seethe with anger. Jealousy, with a hint of hatred, would describe Raymond's feelings for this favourite son.

"Get out of here!" Raymond yelled, as he chased Larry through the back porch of the small, two storey, stucco covered house. The kitchen door slammed shut behind them.

How can I get myself into so much trouble and I haven't even talked to Allen, yet?

He always had trouble with Allen. Allen meant well, but Raymond resented this slightly-built, blond, white man who had married his mother. He never talked about machines, just computers. Raymond felt slighted, but he still wanted to be left alone to work on his snowmobile. He loved mechanical things and he did well in school where he could work with his hands. He loved his Small Engines and Outdoor Education classes. Math and Social Studies were okay, but his heart wasn't in it. Allen always got on his case about doing better in school. His real dad didn't need all that stuff. Raymond went with his dad on the trap line occasionally and he saw how smart he was in the ways of the bush. *Who needs algebra anyway?*

"I guess it was a bad idea to let you get that snowmobile after all," Allen said as he lifted the lid of a pot on the stove. His calm, quiet voice made Raymond want to scream. "It seems like there's nothing but trouble around here since you've been working on that machine. Maybe we'll have to ban you from the garage until your grades improve."

Larry smirked from the stairway. Emily peered sad faced from behind Rose, as she had the grease wiped from her tights.

Rose kept quiet, which was her usual way of dealing with things.

Raymond was ready to throw a major fit and he felt like smashing everything in sight. The smell of a spaghetti supper, with its tangy tomato sauce and garlic dusted bread sticks filled the air, but Raymond knew he couldn't eat here tonight. He turned, slammed the door behind him, and headed into the night. The cold air stung his nostrils, but his head boiled with anger.

CHAPTER 2

Raymond wanted to cry, but he didn't. He had done his share of crying over events of the past and that hadn't really changed anything. Having just turned fourteen, he had done a lot of growing up in the last few months. His muscles were starting to harden on his five foot five inch frame as he headed for six feet. He would look like his father, a big man with black hair, brown skin and a smooth complexion favouring the Aboriginal genes. Would he face discrimination in the future? Even now some people would give him an angry slur or a caustic look, but discrimination usually happened with subtle undertones.

Pulling his collar up around his neck, he headed up the street. For some reason, he turned at the corner and started jogging along the by-pass road that went to Old Town. The name Old Town had come from the Cree village located here long before white explorers "discovered" the Lake. A fierce wind was blowing in from Lesser Slave Lake as he crossed the bridge over the Lesser Slave River. His chest tightened, as his lungs tried to suck in sufficient oxygen. The fall overturn of lake water always produced a dull, musty, swamp smell. The days were getting shorter, the nights longer and much colder, causing the Lake to freeze along the shoreline. Raymond started to run faster when he caught a glimpse of a flickering light coming from Marg's cabin. Marg, an Aboriginal woman, kept the traditional ways and she lived in a log cabin along the river. Raymond didn't believe in all the spirit stuff that Marg talked about, but since she was an elder, he respected her for trying to keep the old customs alive. Marg listened to him and she always had food. Right now, food seemed a lot more important than talk.

Several muskrat and beaver pelts hung from the woodshed. Marg had stretched them on drying boards, which turned the whitish skin, with its streaks of yellow fat and traces of blood, outward and squeezed the soft brown fur inside. The air reeked with the pungent smell of decaying carcasses.

Too old to go out on the trap line anymore, Marg still did some trapping along the river and ox-bow, where she followed a meandering, grass covered path. Raymond knew Marg could teach him a lot about trapping and skinning, but he preferred working on machines because he didn't have to kill anything.

As he got closer to the cabin, the pleasant aroma of moose meat and bannock started triggering his taste buds and his stomach growled with hunger pangs. No one knocked on Marg's door. She welcomed everyone. The muffled bark of a dog gave away Raymond's presence. Storm, Marg's old, docile dog with sad eyes, always wanted some attention.

"*Pe-pihtokwe*," Marg called in Cree. Raymond unlatched the hand carved, wooden latch and stepped inside. "Raymond!" she said in a surprised voice. "Come and eat." She offered him a chunk of fresh bannock and a piece of moose meat.

Raymond managed a muffled, "thank you." His cheeks bulged and his face lit up as he enjoyed the distinct taste of wild game and the smoke tinged flavour of the bannock. Marg mixed another batch of bannock and boiled several more strips of meat. She usually cooked on the old wood cookstove, but now she wrapped some dough on a stick and handed it to Raymond.

"The coals in the fireplace are just right for roasting."

As the fire crackled and periodically spit sparks in his direction, Raymond rotated the stick to bake the bread until it glowed golden brown on all sides.

Marg was a woman of few words, but she was a good listener. Now she started the conversation.

"How's your mom?" Her wrinkled face and gnarled hands showed the years of living in the bush and on a trap line. Raymond thought her smile seemed to anticipate his answer.

"Okay." Marg usually asked about his mom, but he thought it was more of a signal for him to start talking than a serious question.

"I finally convinced Mom and Allen to let me buy a snowmobile, but now it seems like they're trying to take it away from me. We had another big fight and I took off."

"That's why you're eating all of my moose meat," Marg chuckled softly.

After a few more bites and a long silence, Raymond opened a touchy subject. "What was my dad like when he lived in town?" Raymond wasn't at all sure he wanted to hear the answer.

"Your father Johnny is a good man with a big heart and he loves you very much, but he hated living in town."

"Mom says he is a drunk. Is my dad a drunken Indian?" Raymond knew this was a delicate question, but, with his hunger subsiding, he figured he could handle it.

"Your father, like many of our people, was forced to leave

his family when he was very young to attend a residential school. Alcohol became a way to cover the pain."

Marg made a perfect slice with her skinning knife through the skin of a beaver, which was lying belly up, on the rough lumber floor. Stale smelling blood oozed from its mouth. With great skill, gained from years of experience, she peeled the skin away from the carcass and started telling Raymond stories about his mother Rose and her family. Rose's father, Raymond's grandfather (*mosôm*), was Alphonse, a great hunter and trapper.

"He made people laugh with his dog team stories. His white, lead husky, Shadow, was always the smartest dog in the bush. He either had to be the most intelligent dog alive or a spirit dog to do all the things your grandfather claimed he could do." Raymond realized Grandfather and Father were men he could be proud of.

"We need water," Marg said as she motioned for Raymond to get the bucket from the shelf. When she flipped the skin so the fur was facing inside against the drying board, Raymond could see tears in her eyes.

"Mother said Grandfather just disappeared. How could that be?"

Raymond shivered, as he and Marg followed the winding pathway to the river. His thin jean jacket was no match for the cold, crisp night air. Stars danced in the black sky above. A tingling sensation spread through Raymond as he heard the rippling of the river and smelled the wood smoke from the fireplace. Marg continued talking as they braced against the cold wind. "Alphonse was a great elder of his people and he had the only trap line on Dog Island. During winter, strong winds can cause a whiteout on the lake and the mainland disappears. One winter, just before Christmas, your grandfather was out on the trap line and he became lost in a blizzard. We don't know what happened, but his dog team was found freezing and starving several days later at the west end of the lake. Alphonse and Shadow were never seen again." Raymond noticed that her smile faded into sadness.

"Where was Mother?" Raymond asked as he pulled up the bucket, with cold water splashing over the sides.

"Your mother and Johnny were living in Slave Lake at the time, but your father hated it. He wanted to live by the old ways. Your mother hated the old ways and she wanted to live like the white women. After the divorce, your father went back up North to hunt and to trap and your mother went to college. She looked after you on her own, you know."

It felt good to get back inside the warm cabin. Raymond swung the water bucket onto a rustic looking shelf by the well worn, rust stained sink. Marg used a long handled dipper to fill an iron tea kettle and she set it on the stove to boil.

"Mother graduated from college, right?"

"Yes, and then she married Allen when you were eight."

Raymond couldn't understand how his mother could marry a white man and give up her Aboriginal culture.

"Sometimes, I wish I could live up North with Father."

"Now, you listen here. It's best for you to stay with your mother and to get your schooling. I can teach you how to trap and skin a beaver."

Marg had made a pot of tea and she brought Raymond a cup. He didn't really like tea, but he sipped on the brown, bitter tasting brew while he petted Storm, the old, female husky Marg talked to when no one else was around.

"I wish I had a dog like you," Raymond said as he caressed her smooth, white coat. A special bond was developing between them and her searching eyes invited more of Raymond's attention.

"Storm is the last dog of your *mosôm's* dog team," Marg said, as she started skinning another beaver and launched into one of her legends, mostly in Cree, but that was mixed with a smattering of English. Raymond wished he knew more Cree so he could understand all of the story. From what he could understand, he learned the importance of not killing more than you needed to live on, using all parts of the animal and returning some to Mother Earth as an offering of appreciation for the life taken. Marg lit some "sweetgrass" and wisps of the gentle, gray smoke drifted throughout the cabin. Some Alberta Aboriginals used the real sweetgrass in their traditional ceremonies, but Marg burned old man's beard, a local fungus (*wihkimâkasikan*) used by northern Cree.

"Mother says these legends are just Indian spirit garbage."

"I know. She tries to act like a white woman, but she'll always be Cree. You'll always be Cree, too."

"I'm not even supposed to be here."

"Well, you just come here any time you want. Next time you'll learn some more Cree."

Raymond enjoyed filling the broken down, antique wood box with splintered pieces of birch wood, but he suddenly realized it was way past time to be home.

"Wow! It's really late. Thanks for everything, but I have to go. I'm in big trouble now!"

"Say hello to Rose and Allen for me. Tell them to come for a visit some time."

Why would she say that? Raymond knew that would never happen. He grabbed his denim jacket from under a sleeping Storm. A few long, white dog hair hung from his collar. The smell of "sweetgrass" saturated the blue denim and spots of red beaver blood decorated the sleeves.

"Good bye," he called as he gasped the frigid air.

That's funny, he thought, as he ran toward the bridge and home. *Usually Marg asks the questions and I do the talking. This time, I asked the questions and Marg did the talking. Wow, I learned a lot.*

Raymond knew that even though he had problems with Rose and Allen, he looked forward to being home with them and Larry and Emily. He would enjoy a nice warm shower in the morning and he would be glad to see his friends at school. Still, he loved to hear Marg tell the traditional stories and he wished he could live off the land like his father and grandfather did. *Why am I so mixed up? What do I really want?"*

CHAPTER 3

Brrrr!" Raymond shivered. Colder now than when he and Marg had gone for water, Raymond wished for his winter parka. The night air stood still and the crystal clear sky had no clouds in sight. Bursts of light sputtered from the stars and one of the planets glowed its steady yellow shine against the black night. The aurora borealis, known as northern lights, created a spectacular show of light and colour as it spread across the sky. Wave after wave of blue, green and purple light washed against the blackness of space. Everything appeared so close in the northern sky. A sharp crack split the silence and echoed through the night. This happened when ice on the lake expanded, sending a wave of sound crashing through the ice to the shoreline. Raymond caught the fragrant scent of spruce and pine wafting across the lakeshore and realized he was part of the boreal forest. This was his land.

A pall of smoke filled haze hung over the town. Some of the smoke came from the industrial park east of town and some from the exhaust of diesel trucks he heard clattering in the distance. Raymond slowed his pace as he passed a clearing near the road. The oily smell of a lease site and the put-put-put of the pump jack pumping oil out of the ground contrasted with the smooth bubbling sound of the river and the pleasant smell of wood smoke in Old Town. A metal shed, next to the pump, glistened in the moonlight and the bark of the engine echoed off its hollow walls.

I wonder what kind of engine that pump has? What fuel is it using? Maybe some day I'll work in the oil patch. There are lots of high paying jobs for heavy duty mechanics. I could be rich. Now I'm thinking crazy again. Can an Indian have a career with an oil company just like white people? True, Mother has a career, but she gave up her traditional ways. Crazy! Just an hour ago I wanted to live off the land by hunting and trapping. Now I'm thinking like a white man!

Raymond fully recognized the conflict between industrial development and the Aboriginal lifestyle which promoted a forest undisturbed by roads, cut lines, clear cuts and well sites. Why did he have such a conflict between the two cultures? He enjoyed running water from a tap, hot showers, flush toilets, microwaves, televisions, and computers. However, this urge, deep within his being, beckoned him to be one with the forest and its inhabitants. He desired to live in harmony with the land, to face the dangers of the wild and to survive against all odds. Maybe this urge arose from an ancient time when young Aboriginal boys passed from childhood to manhood. Would he be able to meet the challenge and succeed or would he wimp out and be a disgrace to his family?

In Raymond's white dominated world, there didn't seem to be any opportunities to prove himself. Now, a darker, depressing question emerged. *Did Grandfather meet the challenge of life or did he give up?* Raymond had to find out.

A dim light from the kitchen window cast distorted shadows on the sidewalk.

I guess Mother waited up for me again, probably worried about where I've been and what I've been doing.

He knew she loved him and he loved her, but how could she be so overprotective? She always thought he was in trouble, either drinking or doing drugs. He had no intention of becoming part of that scene, but it seemed Mother already had him listed as an addict. The squeaking storm door announced his entry.

Glad for the warmth of the kitchen, Raymond soon shivered from the cold glare of his mother.

"Why were you down at Marg's so long? It's past midnight and you have school in the morning."

"Who said I was at Marg's?"

"Well, the only time you smell like a "sweetgrass"-smoking, dead beaver is when you come home from her place. I told you not to go there to listen to all that spirit stuff. Now go take a shower and get to bed."

As Raymond climbed the stairs, he noticed Allen by the bedroom door.

What does he care?

Why do I want to be involved with the old ways anyway? I'm just a reject.

As the warm water cascaded down his brown body and dripped off his straight, black hair he wondered why his mother had given up the old ways. Why did she rant about him seeing Marg? Maybe she had seen how the clash between the old ways and the modern world had been responsible for capturing so many of her friends and family in a world of alcohol and drugs. Maybe this turned her against Marg and the traditional culture. Maybe she had experienced the hardship herself and didn't want him to fall into the same trap. Wasn't this why she divorced Father? *Can I believe her story?*

The frothing shampoo covered his head. Some ran down his face and stung his eyes. The dead beaver smell seemed to cling to his body. He had to chuckle though, when he pictured a "sweetgrass"-smoking, dead beaver. *Ha! Mother has a sense of humour, even in her anger.*

The warm towel felt good as it caressed his body and a look in the mirror reflected the developing muscles on his tall, lean frame. Could he imagine a headdress and war paint? Would he be brave in battle or a coward?

Maybe, if he listened to Marg, he would try to live by the old ways and become frustrated like Father and maybe Grandfather. *Will I fall into the alcohol trap and end up being a drunk or maybe committing suicide? No! That can't be!*

The bed creaked its familiar chorus as he jumped onto it, pounding his fist into the pillow. A few skinny feathers went floating on the air currents. *Will I end up being like this chicken, whose feathers were plucked to make some rich dude comfortable?*

Why did he want to be involved in the traditional ways anyway? It was a trap! Why couldn't he just leave it alone? Give up the old ways. Deny he was Cree. Get a good job as a mechanic. *Make lots of money. Great future. Be Happy.* The sound of a soft snore filled the room, bouncing off all the accessories common to a white man's world.

CHAPTER 4

On his way downstairs for breakfast, Raymond could hear Larry's squeaky voice.

"How come Raymond gets to stay out all night? I heard him come in after midnight. Aren't you going to do anything about it?"

"Mind your own business!" Raymond snapped.

"Beaver guts on your jacket again, eh?"

"No, it's blood."

"Beaver guts!" Emily chimed in. "Is that the stinky smell?"

"No, that's "sweetgrass" smoke."

"Mommy, Raymond's been smoking."

"Not that kind of smoke. It's used for Indian things."

"Indian things? Like war dances and tom-toms?"

It is no use. They will never understand. Raymond grabbed his overloaded backpack and headed for school, hurting from another misunderstanding with his family.

Raymond did okay, considering the frustrating start to his day. He reviewed his algebra before class and he thought he did well on the chapter test. As usual, his Small Engines class went by too fast. He found a new kind of carburetor adjustment on the Internet and he couldn't wait to try it out on his own.

The weather had turned particularly nasty during the day and on his way home, blizzard winds forced Raymond to hunch forward as he struggled to keep walking.

I'm glad I took my parka this morning. My jacket's full of beaver guts anyway. Ha!

The wind howled around his ears and the snow stung his face. He pulled the hood up over his head and he felt the warm, fur collar against his forehead. This fur had kept some animal warm during winter and now he enjoyed the same comfort. Too bad it had to be killed. Even with the hood pulled up tight, he still had to breathe and the cold air burned as it rushed into his waiting lungs. Every now and then, he turned his head so his nose snuggled into the long hair of the fur, which helped take the chill off the arctic air.

Life is good.

The blowing white snow blurred some of the trees as he walked along the sidewalk toward home. The snow squeaked under his boots and his fingers tingled from the cold, reminding him that winter had come to stay.

This must be like the whiteout Grandfather faced on the island. At least I have a sidewalk to follow.

Home alone after school, Raymond knew Mom would be picking up the others in the Suburban. He grabbed the garbage can and lugged it to the back alley.

Whew! That spoiled hamburger in there smells worse than all of Marg's beaver pelts. He hated this job, but it was his week for taking out the garbage and cleaning the basement.

After a quick change of clothes, Raymond headed for the garage. He wanted to get lots of work done before Larry or Emily got home to bother him. He could hardly wait to start on his carburetor. The feel of the smooth metal and the faint squeal of the screw as he applied pressure with the screw driver, gave Raymond a warm feeling of satisfaction. His adjustments would determine the performance of his machine. *Power!* Could he really give this up to go trapping and killing animals for their fur? This carburetor adjustment would give his old engine a new life. He could feel the acceleration already. *Wow!*

Supper time turned out to be a much more pleasant event than last evening.

Allen came home and announced, "A real blizzard is blowing in from Dog Island. No one goes out tonight!"

"You look like a snowy Sasquatch," Emily teased.

"And now he's going to be a warm, snowy Sasquatch," Raymond said as Allen grabbed Emily and buried his dripping face into her belly, making her laugh.

"Have a look at this," Allen said as he tossed something in Raymond's direction.

Raymond took the envelope and looked inside.

"What is it?"

"See if you can fill it out. You'll need a serial number if you are going to register that piece of junk in the garage."

Raymond had worried about getting his machine insured and registered so he could run it on public land.

Allen must have taken care of this today. Great!

"Thanks," he said as he pulled out the registration form. He would have no trouble finding the serial number.

"How about a game?" Larry called from the computer. Raymond really wanted to read his new copy of *Popular Mechanics*, but he decided to humour Larry a bit. He wanted to get on the good side of Larry, especially since he needed him for a little excursion. Larry would be good company on a snowmobile ride to Dog Island. Raymond needed lots of brownie points.

Even though Raymond tried to win some of the games, he couldn't match Larry.

"Ha! Ha!" Larry gloated.

Good. More chance of a pay off, Raymond thought.

Tantalizing odours wafted in from the kitchen and Raymond could tell Allen was cooking up one of his fantastic Chinese dishes. The braising of the chicken in olive oil with its smoking, searing smell, the simmering of green vegetables, and the robust smell of the garlic and other spices would unmistakably blend into a beautiful combination of flavour, guaranteed to embellish the appetite and ambush the taste buds. Raymond didn't need to embellish his appetite. He headed for the kitchen.

"I'm famished," he said as he lifted a lid.

"Get out of there!" Allen teased.

What a contrast with last night, Raymond thought, as he savoured every part of the meal. *Last night I enjoyed the life of a Native American, eating wild tasting moose meat and smoked bannock in a log cabin and experiencing the old ways of the Cree people. Tonight I am a Native American, eating Chinese food with its hot, spicy qualities and getting pleasure from the tang of plum sauce.*

Raymond cleaned out the wok and devoured the scrapings. He thoroughly enjoyed the comforts of a typical, white Canadian family.

"Mr. Wilmore called today and he said you got ninety percent on your algebra test," Rose said with a smile.

"I guess doing my home work helped a bit."

"You can do it if you just put your mind to it."

"Yes Mom. This is only the billionth time I've heard that."

Mr. Wilmore always gave praise and encouragement to his students.

It sure feels better succeeding than failing. I've done enough of that the last while. Maybe I can pass this course after all.

Raymond helped Mother do the dishes and he kept

bugging her by giving these huge belches. That plum sauce had sure generated a lot of gas.

Life in the white man's world is good, but Marg's world still haunts me, Raymond thought. *What happened to Grandfather? Could he still be living on the island? Did he and Shadow abandon the family? Was Grandfather murdered? If Grandfather was such a great trapper, how did he get lost and why couldn't he find his way home? Had the traditional ways failed him? Had he lost his will to live?* Raymond wanted to ask Mother, but he lost his nerve.

When the dishes were done Raymond headed for the garage. The storm raged across the lake as he ducked in through the side door. Allen had agreed to let him keep a heater running during the coldest weather. It kept the garage from freezing, but not warm. Although his fingers were cool and they felt stiff, he could easily manipulate the tools necessary to put the final adjustment on the carburetor.

Wow! I have enough Chinese gas to fire up this engine on the spot.

Now he had to attach the carburetor to the engine. His hands sensed the correct position and the screws turned gently into their holes. Tightening the last screw with his screwdriver, he stepped back to admire his work. A sense of pride spilled out of his soul. He wanted to try it out right now, but that would have to wait until tomorrow.

As he stepped from the garage into the cold night and headed for the house, the wind howled around him and in a haunting way, he sensed his grandfather calling to him from the island. Now, he knew, he had to visit the island to look for Grandfather.

"I'd like to take a trip to Dog Island to look for Grandfather," Raymond announced as he walked into the living room.

"You what?" Rose sputtered as she leapt out of the big rocker.

"Larry and I could take the snowmobile on an overnight trip and stay on the island for a day or so. We could look around for any sign—"

"You are not going to do any such thing. Marg is filling your head with that spirit talk about Grandfather again, isn't she? Well, you listen to me. You are not allowed to go near that island! Do you hear me?"

"Better listen to your mother," Allen said. "It's pretty dangerous going out on the lake in winter. There may be pockets of open water where methane gas bubbles up from the bottom. Sometimes the top freezes over, but the ice is real thin and a machine will break through and sink."

Raymond knew Allen was right. He had seen people break the ice on some of the small bubbles and light them with a cigarette lighter. Flames would shoot up like a blow torch, flashing their tongues of blue and yellow fire. It would be neat torching one of those big holes. And Mother thought he had a lot of gas.

I don't want to fight tonight, Raymond thought. *Besides, it's too cold to walk out to Marg's.*

"Okay. Goodnight."

The suggestion of taking his snowmobile to the island had brought a storm of protest from Mother and Allen. But why? Mother accused Marg of filling his head with spirit talk and Allen tried to scare him by talking about open water holes. Mother never wanted to talk about Grandfather. Why not? What was she afraid of? Was she hiding a terrible family secret? *I have to find out, even if it means sneaking out to the island.*

"Larry. Are you awake?"

"You're crazy, man," Larry retorted as he awoke from a

light sleep and started comprehending what Raymond had suggested.

"Shhh," Raymond urged.

"Those Indian spirits have you going crazy again. There's no way I'm going to that haunted island."

"Think about it. Maybe you can drive the snowmobile part of the way."

Larry ignored Raymond, rolled over and went back to sleep.

Raymond knew he had failed in his attempt at convincing Larry to go with him to Dog Island, but, at least, Larry could think about it for awhile.

The lights were out, but a fluttering beam danced around Raymond's head as the branches of the tree outside their window swung back and forth in the whistling, winter wind.

The glow from the street light bounced off the purple walls and outlined two single beds squeezed into the small upstairs bedroom. It reflected on a large ceiling poster above Raymond's bed showing a brand new snowmobile flying through the air. Snow was billowing out behind. Raymond could almost hear the roar of the engine. It soon became a purr in the distance as he drifted off to sleep.

CHAPTER 5

After a long day at school, Raymond wanted to try out the reconditioned engine. He adjusted his helmet, tucked the well worn jacket collar underneath and jammed the throttle, peeling a layer of snow off the driveway. Taking the off-road trail, which meant going slow to keep the noise down through town, Raymond finally reached the hills south of Slave Lake.

"Ugundza!" Raymond yelled as the feeling of power surged through his veins. His heart pounded, his head throbbed, and his hands and feet trembled with excitement. How would it perform going up the old ski hill?

Zigging and zagging around stumps and ruts, Raymond, at last, reached the open trail, pointed the skis straight up the hill and throttled the carburetor wide open. Now the adrenalin rush hit him full force. Snow swirled around the speeding machine and the roar of the engine vibrated his black helmet along with every bone in his body. The skis lifted completely off the trail with just the track propelling him up the slope and through the air.

What a rush! This is living. No Math or Science to worry about. Homework will have to wait.

Just as Raymond crested the hill, a racing snowmobile flew past, covering him with snow and gravel from the well worn trail.

"Get that piece of Indian garbage off the trail!" a voice behind a silver helmet screamed.

"I'll race you any day!" Raymond shouted, knowing full well he wouldn't have a chance with his old two-seater.

It didn't make much difference, since the other rider was off in an instant, showering Raymond and his long track snowmobile with gravel.

"Idiot!" Raymond screamed, as a flying rock put another crack in his already battered windshield. His legs started shaking again and his body trembled, but this time from anger, not excitement. His throat tightened as he endured another act of prejudice. He took a time out and stifled his urge to get even.

So my snowmobile isn't a racing machine like the rich kids in town have, but it is mine and I love it. Actually, considering its age, it did a super job climbing that hill. That's when he realized his adjusted carburetor had performed like a brand new one. Not even one sputter.

Raymond's composure returned, as the pride in his mechanical skill sprang from his inner being and a feeling of satisfaction filled him with contentment about being who he was.

"It's okay to be Indian, and you're not garbage," Raymond said as he patted the hood of his snowmobile. He scraped the slush from the windshield, cleaned his face mask, and then he pulled up to the lookout on Rabbit Hill. Rabbit Hill was the popular viewpoint overlooking Lesser Slave Lake, with its miles of sandy beach and the Town of Slave Lake, neatly outlined into different subdivisions. The rounded peak of Marten Mountain, with its soft blue hues, painted a beautiful background. A slight breeze crested the hill and Raymond took off his helmet to let the air blow through his hair and to dry his sweating forehead. The light touch of the wind on his face and the fresh smell coming from the now frozen lake, helped him relax after the incident with the racer. In the distance, Dog Island, with its multi-coloured shades of green and brown, rose out of a sea of white. Drifting snow and a shroud of haze added to its mysterious aura.

Dog Island, a spiral of sand left from a past ice age, now covered with spruce and pine forest, rose out of the depths of the surrounding lake. Big enough to support a homestead in the olden days, it served as a stop for the steamships taking supplies to the Peace River Country and Alaska. The local trappers and the Royal Canadian Mounted Police kept their sled dogs on the island during the summer months, giving it the name, Dog Island.

Is Grandpa still on the island? Why didn't he return? Is the haze a bad omen? Why are Rose and Allen so afraid of it? The only way to find out is to go to the island and see for myself.

"Enough of this!"

Raymond jumped on his machine, snapped his helmet shut and throttled a start, making a sweeping trail around the parking lot and nearly running into a parked car.

What's a car doing over here? The cemetery. A lady was standing by a tombstone. Who was it? Did she lose a father? A mother? A baby?

What was it like for Rose to lose her father? Raymond could almost feel the loss of a father. In a way he had lost his father. He rarely saw him. A twinge of grief gripped Raymond in the stomach. What was it like to die? Where would he be buried if he died? Here in the white man's cemetery on top of Rabbit Hill, or with his grandfather at the Aboriginal burial ground in Old Town? *Grandfather!* Grandfather wasn't buried. Or was he? And Grandmother. Where was she? Rose and Marg never mentioned a grandmother. Was she dead or alive?

I'm so mixed up? I don't belong anywhere.

"Aarrgh!" Raymond screamed as he spun gravel behind the accelerating snowmobile. He wanted to get out of there as soon as possible.

It's supper time and I'm starving.

CHAPTER 6

F ire!" Emily shrieked as she burst in from the garage.
"Snowmobile's on fire."
Raymond jumped to his feet and homework papers

went flying everywhere. No time for a coat. He braced against the blast of frigid, arctic air and bolted for the garage, T-shirt flapping from side to side. His throat choked with fear as he expected to see flames leaping from his masterpiece. To his relief, only curls of steam rose from under the hood as the warm engine cooled in the cold air.

"Emily, you little brat. Why did you yell, fire?"

"I saw flames and smoke," Emily said as she came back to the garage.

"You did not."

"Did so."

"Maybe someone should torch it," Larry cut in. "Just a piece of Indian garbage."

"Get out of here!" Raymond screamed. A wave of depression started building in the pit of his stomach. *Even my own family despises me because I'm an Indian.*

Raymond started chasing Larry, ready to beat him to a pulp, and then he remembered his plan. *I need Larry whole, not pulverized.*

"Fire. See, fire is coming out of here." Emily pointed to the steam rising from the hood.

"That's okay. It's just steam. Thanks for letting me know."

Raymond laughed as he realized what Emily saw. He had put decals on the hood showing flames shooting out of the engine. These, along with speed stripes made it look cool. However, Emily saw steam coming up past the hood and it looked like smoke pouring out of the flaming decals. It looked real to her.

Realizing the cold, Raymond scooped Emily up in his strong arms and swung her back and forth as they bounced into the house. He loved to hear her laugh.

"Run," he teased, as he put her down and chased her into the living room.

Larry was sprawled on the floor in front of the TV.

"How would you like to drive a piece of Indian garbage?" Raymond asked as he walked passed.

"Sure. When do we go?"

"As soon as the home work's done."

"I'll get dressed."

Raymond knew it would be okay to take a short night run after supper as long as he had his homework done. He would be extra cautious with Larry along, but he wanted to spring his newest idea on him.

The snowmobile had cooled down, but it still fired up on the first pull. The boys turned it around, tightened their helmets, and headed out of town. Raymond said he would drive first and then, he would let Larry take over later. Larry laughed as he bounced on the seat behind. A good sign.

The headlight opened the darkness and the roar of the engine made beautiful music. The wind blew cold, even behind the face mask and ridges of frost started to build up along the edges. The pungent smell of the exhaust, mixed with his damp, sour breath inside the helmet, made a strange concoction of odours. On occasion, the warm breath would fog up the inside of the visor, making it difficult to see. The element of surprise also heightened the thrill of the chase, since each bump on the trail launched the snowmobile in a different direction.

Raymond stopped along a straight stretch of the trail to let Larry take his turn at driving. Later, he could tell from the bubbly giggling and bursts of laughter coming from under the helmet that Larry loved to drive.

"Take a left at the cut line!" Raymond yelled next to Larry's helmet. "We'll head to the jack pines."

"Are we going to party?" Larry yelled back with a grin.

Before long, the headlight lit up the gnarly, curved trunks of the jack pine trees. The machine snaked its way in and around the different groves, staying on the trail to preserve the fragile under story. The old man's beard, a greenish gray, stringy lichen, hung in long flowing clumps and every now and then it wrapped around their helmets as the snowmobile sped under the branches. Raymond reached up from his spot behind Larry and cleared off a soft, yet abrasive, pine scented, tangled mass. It reminded him of a Halloween haunted forest with its shadows and distorted figures changing shape as the headlight bounced and turned. The engine performed flawlessly and the next cut line provided a welcome escape from this spirit world.

"You take it!" Larry said as he hopped off and pulled clumps of lichen from around his neck. "Let's get out of here!"

"I'm going to stop at Marg's for a minute," Raymond said.

"Not at that spirit woman's place. I've had enough spirit stuff from going through that haunted forest."

"It's okay. We won't stay long, and besides, she might have something to eat. Come on."

Raymond tried to ease the throttle as he pulled into Marg's yard, but when he turned the engine off, the silence was deafening. The head light died out and the pitch black night closed in around them like the quiet of death. As their eyes adjusted to the night, a faint light flickered from a lantern inside the log cabin. Raymond opened the door a crack and asked, "Marg?"

"*Pe-pihtikwe*"

"I guess you knew someone was coming," Raymond said sheepishly.

"Couldn't miss it."

Half in and half out of the door, Larry hesitated, not sure he wanted to come in. Storm snuggled up to Raymond's leg.

"Come on in and shut the door," Raymond said, as he petted the dog with the searching eyes.

"It stinks in here," Larry muttered.

"It's moose meat cooking."

"Have some bannock," Marg offered as she continued sewing beads on a moccasin. "Moose meat too." She motioned to the pot on the wood cookstove.

"Thanks," Raymond replied while he stuffed his mouth with the golden warm bread and grabbed a slice of meat to go with it.

"Are you sure this is moose meat? It looks like beaver guts to me," Larry whispered to Raymond.

"You boys sure made a lot of noise when you came this time and you smell bad too."

Raymond realized that the caustic smell of snowmobile exhaust made a sharp contrast with the pleasant smell of bannock. He helped himself to more bannock and he fished out another piece of moose meat. He had to laugh when he saw Larry munching down his second piece.

"Pretty good beaver guts, eh?"

"Not bad when you're starving."

"Your grandfather never used a machine," Marg said as she got up from her beading to add a piece of wood to the cookstove. "He always said, 'machines may die, but dogs will run for ever.'"

"What does that mean?"

"Well, if your snowmobile quits when you're on the trap line, you may freeze to death, but if you have dogs, they'll always bring you home."

"Then, why didn't Grandfather's dogs bring him home?"

"Maybe they did."

Marg picked up something shiny from a shelf and handed it to him.

"Here, this is your grandfather's tinderbox."

"What's it for?"

"It's for making fire when you don't have matches."

Raymond cracked open the lid of the round, palm-sized, metal container and peered inside. He could see a pile of black, charred fungus in the middle and a small, flat rock on one side.

"What is this stuff?"

"It's tinder. Here, let me show you."

Marg proceeded to make sparks by striking her hunting knife against the small rock. One of the sparks landed on the mushroom charcoal, made by burning it in the absence of air. She grabbed a pile of cattail straw from the wood box and scraped the glowing ember onto it. Enclosing the ember with straw, she held it in her hand and swung it around in the air until it started to smoke. Marg began to blow on the smoking straw between her hands and it soon burst into flame. She threw it into the fireplace before it burned her hands.

"That's how your grandfather made fire without matches."

"How did you get Grandfather's tinder box?"

"Your grandfather gave it to me."

Taking a small cloth pouch closed with a draw string, she opened it and pulled out a mixture of dried leaves.

"This is also your grandfather's."

Raymond smelled the leaves and recognized some Labrador tea leaves mixed in with others he didn't know.

"Grandfather used this for tea?"

"Yes. It makes good tea. Now it's yours. Take it."

Raymond put the leaves back into the pouch, crammed things back into the tinder box and worked the lid back and forth until it was tight. He didn't really want these things, but he couldn't hurt Marg's feelings so he stuck them into one of the deep side pockets along the leg of his pants.

"Don't take that stuff," Larry whispered. "It's witch doctor poison."

An overwhelming sense of confusion gripped Raymond. He had to get out of here. He grabbed Larry, as he started for another piece of bannock, and headed him out the door.

"Thanks, Marg. Sorry for the noise and the smell."

The black of the night matched the depth of the winter cold and a deep, dark emptiness hit Raymond right in the middle of a piece of swallowed moose meat. The feeling came quite often lately. This tearing feeling seemed to rip his insides apart. One part went with the old ways, the other went to the modern ways.

Some relief came as the engine jumped to life on the first pull. *What a machine.* He would never be stranded by his machine. He'd know how to fix it. At least it wouldn't run away. Hadn't the dogs run away on Grandfather? Left him to die? Where was he? How could he just disappear? Why did Marg have his Grandfather's tinder box? Was Larry right about the witch doctor connection?

The way home blurred for Raymond as he ran on automatic. Larry had a great time bouncing around on the seat behind.

"We should do this again sometime," Larry said as they pulled the snowmobile into the garage. "Not the spirit woman thing. I mean running the snowmobile."

For a moment, Raymond didn't believe his ears, but then he snapped alert.

This is it. Now!

"Maybe we could take the snowmobile to the Wilderness Camp some weekend. The cabins have bunk beds and wood heaters. It would be easy to ride on the lake most of the way and then head south through the bush to the camp."

"Sounds like fun," Larry said. "Would Mom and Dad allow us to go?"

"Maybe if we both work on them."

"Bedtime!" Rose called, as both boys came in from the cold.

Raymond could hardly contain himself. Larry had

taken the bait. A little detour to Dog Island on the way to the Wilderness Camp wouldn't hurt anyone and if he could convince Larry not to tell, no one would ever find out. He had to see the island for himself and this seemed like the only way to do it. Maybe, then, this haunting feeling would go away.

CHAPTER 7

"We can go? Thank you, Mom! Thank you, Dad!" Raymond beamed.

"Yahoo!" Larry chimed in.

"Not so fast!" Allen replied. "You have lots of work to do first!"

"I don't want you to go," said Emily, close to tears. "You might get eaten by a bear."

"Don't worry," Raymond reassured her. "Bears are sleeping now and even if a bear does come out of its den, we'll be safe in the cabin."

"You could take a great big gun and shoot him dead and make bear soup and make a bear skin rug and——." She skipped off to play hunting. Actually, Raymond didn't like shooting things, especially out of season, even though treaty Indians had the right to kill for food any time.

Wow! Things were definitely falling into place. A month ago, this seemed impossible. Now his parents had just agreed to let him go to the Wilderness Camp and Larry wanted to go along.

Then Raymond realized he had joined Larry and Emily in calling Allen "Dad". It sounded okay and it seemed right at the time, yet Allen was not his dad, but he seemed like a dad and he wasn't even Cree.

Why am I so mixed up? Aarrgh!

The next two weeks, the boys spent time planning and preparing for the trip. Raymond had been to the Wilderness Camp before on a Cadet trip, but had never approached it from the lake side. They had crossed the Swan River on a swinging bridge and hiked in along a tractor trail. It would be a little more difficult to find the camp from the lake, especially when the land marks were covered by snow. They would have to follow the shoreline most of the way. Of course, he would have to go over the open part of the lake to get to Dog Island, but that would just be a quick detour. The rest of the time, they would stay close to the shoreline.

"We should get a map of the Slave Lake region," Raymond said to Larry as he painted the last side of his new tool box. "We can go to the Forestry office tomorrow and pick up one."

Raymond had been doing a lot of planning for this trip. He had built a tool box at school and had bolted it onto the back of his snowmobile. They could carry their sleeping bags, valuable first aid equipment and tools inside. He even had a lock on the latch. Raymond was proud of his design. It fit perfectly and the new black paint made it blend into the back of the snowmobile just as if it had come from the factory. It cost a lot less, too.

Let's see, a sharp axe, water proof matches, flashlight, hunting knife and twine. Snowmobile suit and boots, sleeping bag, insulated underwear and, oh yes, toilet paper. Lots of toilet paper.

"Exactly when are you leaving on this winter safari?" Rose asked in a rather subdued manner. Raymond hadn't noticed her enter the garage.

"Next Friday is teachers' in-service and we have the day off. I thought maybe we could start out Friday after lunch. That should give us enough time to get set up in the cabin before dark."

"What about Saturday?"

"We'll just spend some time exploring the area and then come home on Sunday. Don't worry, Mom. We'll be fine."

"I know you will. Just want to make sure you have enough clean underwear." She laughed as she walked away. Raymond watched Rose leave the garage, but he sensed she knew about his plan. *How does Mother know I have another motive for going on this trip? Why did she ask about my plans for Saturday? How do mothers know these things?*

The next night, when Allen came home from work, he tossed a map to Raymond.

"Here you go. See if you can read this map."

Allen and Larry had stopped at the Forestry office. They had picked up a special forest cover map of the whole Lesser Slave Lake area.

"Look at all of the lines on this baby," Raymond remarked.

There were lines marking out the roads, rivers, cut lines, pipelines, well sites and forestry cut blocks. The streams were determined by looking at the contour lines. The closely spaced lines indicated a major drop in elevation with a stream flowing in between two large formations. Dog Island had many interesting features as well.

"Wow! There is some rugged territory south of the lake. I didn't realize we had mountains."

"They are just foothills of the mighty Rockies," Allen noted. "But, they are beautiful and rugged. Just be careful if you decide to explore some of those canyons with the snowmobile. It can be dangerous."

"Emily! What do you think you're doing?" Raymond yelled as he opened the garage door.

"Just checking to see if you have enough toilet paper."

A streamer of toilet paper was wound around every part of the snowmobile. It covered the windshield and the helmets were stuffed with it.

"You little turkey. I'll fix you." Raymond grabbed the end of one streamer and started winding it around Emily. She was kicking, screaming and laughing while toilet paper was flying everywhere. Raymond did a few last windings and then he picked her up and ran for the house. He dropped her on the sofa, just as mother came storming in from the kitchen.

"What on earth is going on in here?"

"I found a mummy on my snowmobile and she came to life."

"Now, I'm a mummy just like you!" Emily squealed with delight.

"Not that kind of mummy," Mother giggled.

What a busy week. The first aid kit had to be stocked with bandages, tape, tweezers for splinters, ointment for burns and, oh yes, a spare flashlight. They needed to buy food. Yes. Food! Eating always seemed to be the best part of a camping trip. The list included sausage, buns, butter, catsup, pancake mix, oatmeal, macaroni and cheese. They needed metal pots for cooking and a small kettle with a handle for boiling water, along with a fry pan and a mess kit with eating utensils.

"Larry!" Raymond called. "What else do we need? I'm sure we forgot something."

The key to winter camping was to pack only essentials, to keep the weight down and to pack everything together to take up the least amount of space. Raymond wanted to have the lunch in an accessible spot, so he would not have to unpack the whole load just to get to the snacks. He knew they would be into the snacks soon after leaving.

What a send off! Allen and Rose came home for lunch on Friday and they gave their last words of warning. Rose gave Raymond a picture letter Emily had made for him at daycare. Toilet paper was streaming out from behind her version of a snowmobile which had stick men for riders.

The cold, clean air made the afternoon sunshine sparkle off the large hoar frost crystals hanging from the shrubs along the beach. Dog Island rose like a forested monument in the distance.

At last! Full throttle ahead!

CHAPTER 8

Raymond's nostrils burned as the cold air rushed by, and the wind chill factor sucked warmth from the centre of his bones. A mixture of white snow and blue smoke billowed out from behind the snowmobile as Raymond pushed the envelope of the new carburetor. The engine roared with power as his thumb pinned the throttle. Pride welled up inside and excitement overwhelmed him.

Maybe I'm not a hunter or trapper, but I sure can fix an engine.

The bright sun never traveled far from the southern horizon at this time of year and reflected glare from the snow and ice glinted off Raymond's helmet visor. The sand dunes along the shoreline receded into a distant backdrop as the skis skimmed across the flat lake. A picture perfect start to a wonderful weekend.

"Slow down!" Larry screamed. "I can't hang on!"

"Don't be such a wimp!" Raymond yelled back through the howling wind.

Small ice ridges formed ripples on the surface and the snowmobile vibrated in rhythm with each ridge.

"I'll dodge the bumps," Raymond laughed, showing off his self confidence.

The skis dug in as Raymond pulled the handle bar sharply to the left and then to the right. The snowmobile swerved in response. It swung the boys from side to side and nearly tipped them over. The feeling of power rose within and Raymond loved every minute of it. Here was his chance to live on the edge.

"Stop!" Larry shrieked from the back. "You're just a crazy Indian!"

"You're just a yellow bellied white man!"

Raymond soon realized he had to be nice to Larry, at least for two days. Besides, it was time for a snack.

"How are you doing?" Raymond asked as he pulled to a stop.

"I've got to pee. I just about lost it in my pants back there."

"Just wanted to put a little spark in your life. Here, have a sandwich." The sticky peanut butter and sweet strawberry jam oozed out over the edge of the crust.

"Where are we, anyway? I thought we were going to follow the shoreline."

"See those trees in the distance? That's Dog Island." Raymond passed Larry a cup of hot chocolate from his thermos bottle. A wisp of sweet smelling steam curled up from the lip.

"You said we were going to the Wilderness Camp," Larry said as he tasted the hot liquid.

"We are, but this is just a little detour on the way. We can make a quick stop on the island, look around, and then head south to Auger Bay. From Dog Island we can follow the landmarks to camp. Have another sandwich."

"I'm not going to that spirit dog place. You're not supposed to go there either. This is just another of your stupid ideas, isn't it?"

Raymond pulled out the map and checked their location.

"Right over here," he said, pointing to the map and sipping the last drop of his hot chocolate. "The island is just ahead and the camp is over here. At this rate we'll be to the island in no time." Raymond didn't really know that, but he had to sound positive.

A sudden gust of wind whipped the map out of Raymond's hand and sent him running after it. The sun had disappeared behind a cloud bank sliding in from the west and the red streaked, purple glow over the lake indicated night would come early.

Raymond shivered. The cold wind cut through his snowmobile suit, but the thought of approaching Dog Island triggered the shiver. Larry was right, but they were getting closer now and he was sure they would have an hour of daylight left to check out the island and still find the Wilderness Camp. One part of him said, "Don't go." The other said, "Go for it."

"Let's go!" Raymond yelled into the wind as he scrunched the map and lunch bag into his backpack.

"We'll never make it! Look at the storm blowing in!"

"We're going to make it! Hang on!"

The snowmobile sprang to life and headed for Dog Island in spite of loud protesting from Larry. A haze shrouded the island and snow spiraled in endless circles around the ominous looking, dark green, tree tops. Raymond no longer tried to avoid the ice ridges. He was in a hurry and they were getting close to the shoreline. Full throttle.

Some ridges had jagged peaks pointing skyward. The snowmobile launched from one peak to the next with a rhythmic thump. Larry screamed for him to stop, but Raymond loved the adrenalin rush surging through his body. *Is this what it feels like to be a warrior on a raiding party, riding a horse at breakneck speed? Would I make a good warrior? Am I brave? Do I have courage?*

Without warning, the next ridge rose out of the haze. Its vertical spires of ice reflected a variety of blue-green hues in the dim light and looked like a crystal chandelier waiting to be smashed. Rising several feet in the air, the snowmobile crunched up one side and launched into the wind. Screaming, yelling and crying rang out through the bleak sky and blizzard winds, but there was no one to hear. Raymond tried frantically to control the machine.

"Water!" Raymond screamed in sheer panic.

"Help!" Larry yelled as he started slipping off the snowmobile when it came splashing onto the open water. Raymond grabbed Larry's arm with one hand and throttled the snowmobile with the other. Its forward momentum and spinning track propelled the machine as it skimmed over the frothing water. Raymond shook with fear and his heart nearly burst from exertion. His muscles ached, but his grip on Larry remained firm. Larry dragged through the water, his legs spread-eagled and completely submerged. His body sprayed water in every direction.

"Aarrgh!" Raymond yelled as he used every last bit of muscle power to steer the machine and to bring it back onto the ice. The skis hit first and they bounced the front end up onto the snow covered, icy shelf. With a roar from the engine and a whir of the track, it rose out of the water. Now, hurtling completely out of control, the snowmobile hit a second, gigantic, ice ridge with a loud, shattering explosion, sending pieces of ice and machine in every direction, while catapulting its riders through the air like rag dolls in a tornado.

CHAPTER 9

"Help! Help!"

I'm dreaming, Raymond thought. *It must be a nightmare.*

"Help! Help!"

It's real. Someone's calling. Larry!

Raymond tried to lift his head. It felt like a ton of bricks. At last, his eyes focused and he discovered himself lying in a crumpled heap on the snow and ice. Cold seeped through his snowmobile suit and some wet spots were soaking his skin. Then, he remembered flying through the air and the terrible crash. *Alive! Thank you helmet.* He shook the snow out of the visor and slowly pulled himself to his feet. *So far so good. A few scratches and a little bit of blood. No broken bones.* He felt numb from the bruising and the cold, but he would be okay.

"Larry! Where are you?"

"Ouch! Owww!" Larry cried in pain from the other side of the crashed snowmobile.

"Coming!"

Tears started flowing and panic crept into Raymond's throat. His prized machine lay sprawled on the ice, a crushed piece of junk. It might never run again.

How bad is Larry hurt? How are we going to get home? I'm scared.

Raymond knew he had to be brave and courageous now. Their lives depended on it.

"What's wrong?" Raymond asked in a thin, trembling voice.

"I can't get up. I think I broke my leg. Owww!"

Another wave of panic swept over Raymond. It started deep in his stomach and rose to his chest with a crushing feeling that strangled his very spirit. His head pounded and he wanted to run away. But where could he run to? They were on Dog Island, miles from home and no way to get there, but to walk.

Walk! Can Larry even crawl? No one will come looking for us. We're supposed to be at the Wilderness Camp. And the island. What about the spirits on the island?

"Help me!" Larry cried again. "I can't get up! I-I'm cold!"

"I'm coming!"

Whether from courage, from bravery or just from common sense, Raymond knew he had to take charge and help Larry. *How much blood? Is it spurting? Check for a broken leg. First priority. Get Larry out of the wind. Keep him warm and dry to prevent hypothermia.*

When Raymond felt Larry's leg through a rip in the pants, he could tell it was broken, but the bone had not punctured the skin. A cut on Larry's leg was bleeding, but not spurting. Larry was not going to bleed to death. Larry shivered and cried out when Raymond tried to straighten the leg.

"Here, put your arm over my shoulder. I'll help you walk, but don't step on your broken leg."

"Owww! I can't! Larry screamed."

"Yes, you can! We'll go over to that fallen tree on the beach. It's not far. You can make it."

The two boys, with their arms around each other and with Larry doing a distorted hop, made their way through the blowing snow to the edge of the lake. A large spruce tree had recently fallen near the shore and Raymond knew it would provide shelter from the wind, as well as a ready supply of firewood.

Concentrating on helping Larry, who was injured and soaking wet, Raymond forgot his own problems and the panic attack disappeared. When they got to the fallen tree, Raymond cleared the snow, broke off a few branches and laid them close to the tree, out of the wind.

"Careful. Lie down here." Raymond tried to support Larry's leg with a long branch, but it only brought on more screaming. "I'll be right back."

Raymond knew that hypothermia, the silent killer, could kill Larry. If his core temperature went below normal, the body systems would start to shut down. Raymond had to move fast. He couldn't let Larry die. *My brother in a casket? No!*

Steam fogged up the inside of his visor. Sweat poured down his face and soaked his shirt. He needed to find his woolen toque and get out of his helmet.

Where are the matches? First aid box? Food?

Although the tool box had broken loose from the snowmobile and had been hurled some distance from the rest of the wreck, it had survived. Raymond headed for the box. *This can be a life saver. Yes!* However, when he passed the loose skis lying on the snow and saw the track spun half off the machine, the finality of the crash sank in. A wave of depression made him want to throw up. *Larry in a casket? Me in a casket? No! I don't want to die!*

Raymond looked in the box and faced another depressing sight. Food, first aid supplies and survival equipment were all mixed together to make a tangled mess. At least it was all there. Raymond grabbed the woolen toques and sleeping bags. He had to get Larry into a sleeping bag and to get a fire going as soon as possible. Raymond hardly noticed the blizzard force winds blowing across the lake. Overexertion kept him warm for now, but he craved a warm drink and food. *Later.*

Snow piled up in front of his boots as he struggled against the wind and searched for the trail leading to Larry under the tree.

"Owww!"

That's a good sign. At least he's still conscious.

"I'm back."

"Don't leave me on this spirit island to die."

"You're not going to die. We'll get you feeling better in no time. Here, let me help you take off your helmet and put on your toque."

Raymond opened one of the arctic sleeping bags and put it over Larry as a temporary measure until he could get a fire going and get the wet pants off the injured leg. He tried to check the twisted leg, but Larry wouldn't let him get a good look. At least the bleeding had stopped and that was a good sign. In any case they were stuck here for the night.

"I'm not leaving you, but I have to go back to the crash before it gets too dark."

"I don't want to stay here alone! I'm scared!"

"Don't worry! You'll be okay! I'll be right back!" Raymond was scared too, but he headed toward the crash site.

A true northern blizzard began to sweep across the lake and the crash scene would soon disappear from view. Raymond struggled with his heavy boots that were warm when riding on a snowmobile, but they were too heavy for walking through deep snow.

Grandfather and Father would have moccasins and snow shoes. I wish I had a pair now.

Raymond grabbed a few essential pieces of equipment from the wreckage, stuck them into the tool box and heaved it up onto his shoulders for the energy sapping hike back to the fallen spruce tree.

"I-I'm-m c-c-cold!"

"I'll get you some hot chocolate," Raymond said as he dropped the heavy tool box. "The thermos is dented, but it's not leaking."

Larry's slurred speech begged for a hot drink, but even this was a good sign in a way. In extreme hypothermia, a person started to feel hot and began to undress. Raymond chuckled at the thought of seeing Larry whipping off his clothes on a spirit filled island in the middle of a blizzard.

Using the small flashlight on his key chain, Raymond

found the emergency lantern. The big beam lit up the scrambled mess inside the tool box. He started to sort out some equipment still intact after the crash and he began thinking about surviving the night.

Here is the thermos. A quick hot drink will help me carry out the heavy work ahead.

Hot chocolate splashed into the cups. Larry slurped his, trying to cool it for drinking. Raymond savoured the moment with his drink. The smell and taste of the sweet drink stirred his hunger for a sandwich dripping with jam. *Later.*

"This may hurt, but we have to take off your wet boots and clothes."

"Owww!" Larry screamed. "My leg!"

Raymond pulled Larry out of his wet clothes, put a temporary bandage on his cut and got him into his sleeping bag. Larry wailed with every movement. The swollen leg looked gross. *I'll have to put a splint on this leg. Later!*

The spruce tree provided some essential materials for surviving the night, but they needed more. Taking the axe he had found, before the blizzard had covered it, Raymond pushed through the deep snow looking for basic shelter and fire building materials: birch bark peeled from a young birch tree, dried cattail stems, old man's beard hanging from a dead spruce, a sturdy young poplar tree for a ridge pole, other saplings and spruce boughs for the top of a lean-to and several dead spruce and poplar logs to build a heat reflector.

After several trips, Raymond dropped in the snow, exhausted.

Just lie down. Take a little nap. No! Keep going. Start a fire.

CHAPTER 10

Cough! Cough! Raymond's eyes burned from the acrid smell. Tears ran from his eyes. Snot dripped from his nose and ran along his lips. The taste of salty slime increased the wrenching of his stomach.

"Don't you know how to start a fire? All you can get is smoke. I'm cold. Owww!" Larry cried. We're going to die on this island, aren't we? Just like your grandfather!"

Cough! Cough!

Raymond tried to ignore the babble coming from Larry, but the mention of his grandfather renewed his own fear. The curse of the island burned within. His fingers trembled and his legs started shaking as he fumbled with the water proof matches. *Why can't I start a fire?* It worked a lot better on the Outdoor Education trip. Last spring the flames leapt from the dry kindling. Now there was only smoke from the cold, wet fuel. Maybe it was the birch bark. He remembered Marg saying that she never used birch bark to start a fire because of some traditional taboo. Tears filled his eyes again and they weren't all from the smoke.

Match after match, but still no fire. Then there was one match left. This one had to work. *Blow! Blow!*

Out! The fire is out. No point in blowing anymore. Snow! Cold! Wind! We're going to die. No!

In his despair, Raymond dropped to his knees. *What's this? My pocket. What's this in the bottom of my leg pocket? The tinder box! Grandpa's tinder box. Can I make fire with this? Marg showed me how, but will it work for me?*

It had to work. The silver box flashed in the beam of the flash light. Raymond turned open the lid and exposed the black fungus. His hunting knife struck the rock several times. One of the sparks hit its mark and began to produce a glowing ember. *How can this make a fire when a whole box of matches didn't work?*

"You're not using that medicine man fungus, are you? Owww!" Larry moaned. "We're going to die!"

Raymond reworked his pile of fire-making sticks, and got them ready to receive the burning cattails. Following Marg's example, he placed the ember into a handful of crushed cattails. Enclosing it in his hand, he started swinging it around and around. Smoke began pouring out. Just as the heat started burning his hand, he placed the hot, smoking cattails into the pile of kindling and started blowing a gentle stream of air into it.

Patience and perseverance paid off. A weak flutter of a flame rose from the pile of cattails, birch bark, old man's beard and dead spruce twigs. Raymond teased the flutter with a light, steady breath and the small flame became a strong, crackling fire. Larger branches fed the fire until at last the flashing flames spread their warmth to the cold, shivering boys. Dead spruce branches burst into flame, showering light and sparks into the face of the blizzard, pushing back the dark of the night.

Grandpa's tinder worked!

***

Live, green branches from the spruce tree enclosed the lean-to and covered the snow base. Larger logs behind the fire pit reflected heat into the lean-to and the boys huddled together in their sleeping bags. Wet clothes hung on branches around the fire. Two sticks splinted Larry's broken leg.

Raymond broke open some smoked sausage and started roasting it over the campfire. The sizzling of the fat and the smoky smell of the charred drippings, heightened his appetite. Raymond enjoyed his first taste of warm food since he had left home and he offered Larry a bite, but Larry was in too much pain to be hungry.

Remembering Grandpa's tea, Raymond hung a small kettle of water over the fire until it boiled. He dumped in some leaves from Grandpa's pouch and soon he had a mint smelling tea brewing.

"Here, have some medicine man tea," Raymond said as he handed Larry a cup of tea and he poured one for himself.

Raymond sipped from his cup. *Not bad for Indian medicine. Maybe Grandpa's medicine will ease the pain and give us both some sleep.*

Raymond had piled branches and wood close to the fire pit and within reach of his sleeping bag. The fire thawed out the frozen wood, making it easier to burn and he could feed the fire without getting cold. He checked to make sure the wood pile would not accidently catch on fire and burn up the lean-to. Dead spruce branches added now and then, burst into flame, painting the camp site with strokes of yellow light. Larger pieces of wood produced a steady source of heat and the coals kept the fire alive until he added wood the next time.

"Wooooo! Woooooo!"

"What was that?" Raymond yelled as he turned to look in the direction of the haunting sound.

"Owww!" Larry screeched. "I'm scared! Spirits! That's what it is. Indian spirits."

"It sounds like a coyote or a dog," Raymond said, trying to disguise his fear.

"Owww! Are there wolves out here? They're probably just waiting to rip us apart. They'll take me first, won't they? They always take the injured prey first. I don't want to be ripped apart by a wolf pack. Owww! I hate you for bringing me out here to die."

"Shut up! You're not going to die. It's probably just a coyote. It won't attack us. It's just checking out the fire to see what's happening in its territory."

"Woooooo! Woooooo!"

Loud and right next to camp, the howl echoed through the rustling bushes. Both boys sat up in surprise and Raymond grabbed a chunk of wood.

"Aaarrgh!" he screamed as he flung the wood in the

direction of the moving branches. Immediately something bolted through the brush. Larry covered his head and he continued his moaning, groaning and crying. Raymond grabbed a bunch of spruce boughs and threw them onto the fire. The flames leapt high above the fire pit and sparks streaked into the air, soon to be lost in the wind and snow of the blizzard. Raymond felt the pulse pounding in his head as he waited for the attack from the pack. It never came.

Larry continued to cry and to complain, but the sleeping bag muffled the sound. Raymond curled up inside his sleeping bag with his head tucked in to mask the tormenting screech of the wind. The smell of sweat and wet socks almost made him puke. Fear of his situation caused his stomach to curl into knots and to churn from side to side. Sheer fatigue gradually overtook all fear and a fitful sleep fell over the campsite.

Maybe the tea will help bring pleasant dreams.

CHAPTER 11

Hike! Get up!" Raymond yelled his commands to a dog team. *But whose dog team is this? Why am I the dog musher? Who is in the basket?*

The gang line strained under the surge of muscle power produced by the pumping legs of the sled dogs. The lead dog, a white husky, kept the gang line taut and the harness of each dog spread the tug lines as they provided motion to the connected sled. The runners skimmed across the packed snow of the trail. Crouching low on the foot pads, Raymond twisted the rawhide covered handle bow and called out, "Haw!" The white husky.... *Could that be Shadow?....* responded immediately and swung the team sharply to the left. The upright stanchions of the sled creaked under the pressure as the sled skidded around the corner. Raymond screamed with delight as the wind ruffled the fur on his hat and flapped the fringes on his beaded moose hide jacket. His mukluks provided the grip needed to maintain his balance on the sled. The frosty breath wisped away from dogs and rider as they glided gracefully across the frozen lake. No engine noise or putrid smoke to disturb the pristine wilderness. *Beautiful!*

A groan came from the basket. Larry moaned in pain from his injuries.

Get up! Faster. Have to get Larry to a doctor.

A sharp whistle from Raymond prompted Shadow to provide leadership to the team. Confidence exuded from driver and lead dog, demanding respect from the other dogs. The team dogs responded to Raymond's call with renewed strength and the wheel dogs were quick to avoid the sled pursuing them from directly behind.

"Water!"

"Geeee!" Raymond's words were lost in the flurry of snow and the scraping of runners on the ice as the sled skidded left while turning to the right. Every dog was bent to the task of carrying out the command to turn right. Too late. The runners dug into an ice ridge and the sled leapt into the air, twisting and rolling. A tremendous splash sprayed water everywhere. The bridle snapped under the strain and cut the sled loose from the dogs. The sled, with its passengers, floated for a brief moment, then started to sink from the weight of the snow hook. Usually used to anchor the team in the snow when the sled stopped, it now anchored the sled to the bottom of the lake.

"Aaarrrgh! Larry!"

His face was wet, but he could breathe. The wetness was coming from a salivating tongue. Shadow was licking his face. He was alive, but how?

"Larry! Where are you?"

"He's over here," a deep voice resonated through the frigid landscape. "Wet, but safe. I guess you need a few more lessons on driving a dog team."

"Grandpa! What are you and Shadow doing here?" His excitement bubbled over. *Can this actually be Grandpa? How can this be true? Grandpa is supposed to be dead.*

"Shadow! Stop licking me." When Raymond opened his eyes he saw only a campsite covered in snow with no tracks of any kind. He shivered. The fire was out, but there were still a few glowing embers. A faint glow of light in the eastern sky indicated the coming of a new day. Blizzard winds still howled overhead. Raymond shook his head, trying to shake off the scary events of the night. His hands trembled with fear. *Island spirits! A spirit dog team! Shadow! Grandpa! What is going on?*

Larry groaned, but he didn't respond to Raymond's call.

Maybe he has internal injuries, as well as a broken leg.

Gut wrenching fear grabbed him from inside and he knew he and Larry had to get off this island. *Now!*

Raymond poked at the fire and he blew a fragile flame from the coals. A larger fire soon spread warmth to the campsite. He dragged himself out of his warm sleeping bag and he put on the partially freeze dried snowmobile suit and boots. Shivering from cold and fear, he decided to try to find the hood of the snowmobile. He made his way through the white fury, trudging along toward the crash site.

Yes! Here it is.

With the hood, some willow boughs and a rope, he started to fashion a sled for Larry. He would be the dog team and he would pull Larry home. He didn't know how he would find his way in the blizzard, but he could tell the general direction from where the sky was getting light and he would strike out toward the East. Courage slowly replaced fear.

"Larry. Have some tea. We have a long trip ahead. We're going home."

"Owwww! I'm not going," Larry said in a delirious manner, as he slurped some of the warm tea.

"Oh yes you are," Raymond said as he unzipped Larry's sleeping bag. "Let me check your leg." Larry still had pain, but the splint and bandage looked okay.

"Owwww! It hurts. I'm cold. How can I walk home?"

"You're not. Here, let me zip this up again to keep you warm. Help me slide the hood under you.

"I can't!"

"Sure you can. We'll put your legs out the back and lash them to this willow sled I roped onto the hood. These spruce bows and your snowmobile suit will act like a pillow."

Raymond had made a makeshift harness from some rope and straps he had found in the tool box and he attached them to the hood with a crude bridle and gang line. This way, he could walk with his arms free and he would pull the home made sled like a sled dog.

Raymond tucked some food, the thermos bottle, and other essentials into the hood. Even a roll of toilet paper went along. With Larry strapped on, Raymond bid farewell to the campsite. *What a beautiful site!* It would hold memories forever. He knew he would return again under more pleasant circumstances. *Will I ever see Grandpa and Shadow again?*

CHAPTER 12

"Hike!" Raymond told himself. Larry's weight bogged him down and the fresh snow kept piling up in front of the hood. Unpredictable gusts of wind came from every direction. Sometimes, the blowing snow caused a complete whiteout. For a while, he could still see the island behind him, and he used it as a guide to head for the mainland.

"Owwww!" Larry moaned. "I'm cold. We're going to get lost on the lake and end up dead like your grandfather."

"It's okay. We'll be fine. Sorry about your leg, but we'll soon get you to the hospital and they'll set it. You'll be as good as new in a couple of years."

"A couple of years! Oh no! I'll never be able to walk again." He started to cry.

Raymond wanted to cry, too. Even though he tried to sound positive, he had no guarantee that Larry would be okay. Maybe they would end up like Grandpa and Shadow, either dead or as spirits on Dog Island.

This whiteout is lasting too long. Can't see the island. Can't see anything. The wind is so strong. I'm so tired. Maybe I should lie down and have a rest. Which way to home? I can't go any farther. We're going to die. I don't want to die. His jaw tightened with determination.

"Hike!" The command was clear and decisive. "Get up."

Raymond immediately snapped the tug line taut. The sled responded to the power from the gang line. "But which way?"

"Come haw!" Grandpa's voice rang out through the blizzard.

That's the wrong way, Raymond thought. *That's going back where we came from. We'll be lost forever now.*

Snap! His harness tightened and it jerked him around. *How can this be happening? What is that up ahead? A lead dog. Shadow!*

Shadow took the lead and Raymond could feel the strength returning to his own weary muscles. His legs became strong as they pumped up and down in the snow and pulled ahead, faster and faster. *Pump the legs. Follow the leader. No looking back. More power when Grandpa yells, 'get up'.* Faster and faster and then everything became a blur. Wind. Snow. Cold. Fatigue. Silence.

***

"Putrid! Gag! Cough! Spit! Shadow's sloppy tongue again." Raymond opened his eyes, shook his head and then heard his mother's voice.

"Wake up, young man. You have some visitors."

"Where am I? Where's Larry? Where's Shadow? Where's Grandpa?"

"Hold everything. Slow down." Larry is in the emergency room. He has a fractured leg and they are checking for internal injuries, but thanks to you and your good first aid work, his leg will be fine. He'll be on crutches and have a cast for six weeks."

"He hates me. Doesn't he?" Raymond began to cry.

"No, he doesn't hate you. He's just glad to be warm for a change. He probably won't go snowmobiling with you for awhile, though." More tears came as Mother pushed the hair out of his eyes.

"Hello, Raymond," Dr. Clinton said as he sauntered into the room. His large hand gripped Raymond's leg and he gave it a good natured shake. "You had a lot of people worried. Just look around. You have a big cheering section. You're quite the hero for getting Larry home alive."

"But, but I didn't...." His voice trailed off. He wanted to tell them about Grandpa and Shadow, and why he didn't get to the Wilderness Camp and.... his eye caught Marg sitting in the corner. *What is she doing here?* He also noticed Allen standing beside her. Surprised to see all of these people, he suddenly realized they all cared about him and they all loved him. More hot tears spilled over his cheeks. *I'm alive. Larry's safe.*

"Well, you take care. You gave us a bit of a scare, but you'll be fine. As soon as you can get up and walk, you can go home. I have to check in on Larry now." The doctor disappeared through the door and Raymond sat up to greet his visitors.

"How did I get here?"

"Well, you dragged Larry and that sled of yours up on the beach," Rose said. "Your grandmother, Marg, found you passed out beside it. She pulled you up to the road and flagged down a log truck driver who used his cell phone to call the ambulance. They brought you and Larry here."

"When we got the call from the hospital, we went to pick up Marg and we came right over," Allen said.

"M-Marg is my grandmother?" Raymond blurted out, not believing his ears.

"Yes, I haven't talked to my mother for years, but you brought us together again," Rose said with a catch in her voice.

"You mean now I can visit Marg whenever I want to?"

"She may not want you to visit that often. At least you won't be bringing that noisy, smelly machine for a while."

"You can come for moose meat and bannock any time," Marg said with a chuckle.

"If you're feeling okay, we'd better take *Kohkom* home," Rose said.

On the way out, Raymond and the others stopped to see Larry. He seemed in good spirits and he even smiled at Raymond. *I guess he's not that mad at me*, Raymond thought.

"We'll come back to get you later," Allen said as they left the room.

Raymond couldn't believe how much all of these people cared for and loved him. Even Allen had tears. *They all love me even if I am a mixed up Indian kid from a mixed up family.*

When they pulled up to Marg's place, there sat the makeshift sled and the harness Raymond had used to pull Larry from the island. He just didn't understand. He was supposed to be a hero, but he didn't even remember getting home. *Is Shadow real or a spirit? What about Grandpa? And Marg is my kohkom? How did she find me? What was she doing out on the lake?*

"Well, this is part of your machine," Allen said. "It still

has its speed stripes and some toilet paper hanging out, but where is the smoke? We'll borrow a snowmobile when this blizzard quits and try to find what's left of yours. It looks like you'll have a little fixing to do."

"I hope the carburetor still works."

Raymond knew he could fix up his snowmobile again. It would take a long time, but he knew he could do it. He also knew he wanted to learn more about the traditional ways and maybe even have a dog team of his own.

Raymond wanted to ask Marg so many questions, but he would have to wait.

"I'll come back tomorrow. I want to learn more about Grandpa and Shadow and maybe start my own dog team."

"Well, I've got just what you'll need."

Marg shuffled off to the cabin and she returned with a fuzzy, white ball of an animal, a beautiful, white husky pup. She handed him to Raymond.

"He is one of Storm's puppies. We'll have to keep him here for a few weeks, but he should make you a good lead dog. He looks just like Shadow, your mosôm's lead dog."

Raymond already knew that.

"Thank you. I love him."

As the puppy licked the tears streaming down his cheeks, Raymond could picture Shadow The Second leading his dog team across the lake to Dog Island. The warm puppy wriggled in his arms. This was not a dream. He was home at last. His spirit deep within was at peace. *I am a great warrior, courageous and brave.* A smile spread across his face, as he handed the puppy back to Marg.